The Other Dimension

Ashwani Kujur

First published by Bumblebee Publishing
Unit of Shree Balaji International
59, N S Road, 3rd Floor, Kolkata - 1

The Other Dimension
Copyright © Ashwani Kujur, 2019

ISBN Print Book - 978-93-5396-427-6

Although the author and publisher have made every effort to ensure the accuracy and completeness of information contained in this book, we assume no responsibility for errors, inaccuracies, omissions, or any inconsistencies herein. Any slights on people, places, or organizations are unintentional.

This book is not based on facts or research.

Author's Note

This book is divided into four 'unequal' parts. Now you must be wondering why so much focus on the word 'unequal'. Believe it or not, there is inequality all around us. Case in point is our lives which are surrounded by inequality at different junctures and phases. This book's theme is fiction, but I would like to leave it to your wisdom to judge if it just a fiction or a metaphor for something more profound. I had to justify the title somewhere, didn't I?

Storytelling is a beautiful art, which has the power to connect people and transcend all banalities of grammar or even realism. We all need a little creativity in our daily lives because we are stuck in this redundant, excruciating robotic lifestyle that we chose, unlike people who stood up, realized, and followed their passion to create something creative every day. Some people find solace in music, sketching, trekking, clicking pictures, cooking or maybe something as simple as sleeping; I, for one have always found comfort in stories, big or small, real, or made up. The idea of different words coming together to create something on a piece of paper that has the power to catapult or suck you into a world where you have never been before gives me butterflies in my stomach.

You might find a lot of discrepancies, some errors or maybe a lot of them. I have attempted to redress them all but in case I have missed it somewhere, all that I can say is I am a story-teller first. Hence, it is totally up to you to finish this book. Sounded rude?

Are you now wondering why should I continue reading this?

Spare a moment! I Got it. Like a true click-baity writer I will list out X reasons why you should continue in your pursuit to finish it:

1. We as humans, find it hard to apologize. For every apology we hand out, there are 10 people who aren't sorry for their actions or words. The world is full of them. We have to learn to handle such situations or people rather than hiding/ avoiding it.

2. We let emotions overwhelm us rather than empowering us.

3. Vibes and energy – we are always surrounded by positivity and negativity; we need to pick it up from the bundle.

4. Gone were the days when people would consume a book of the size of a watermelon. This book is kept short and as simple as possible without compromising on the story-telling.

5. You are powerful- your actions, words or even your silence is powerful. It can move mountains, always remember!

6. We find it hard to forgive people. We are always in a dilemma, should we forgive someone or not.

7. Lastly, this is not a self-help book that is meant to cash-in on your insecurities and make you feel you are missing out on something.

It's going to be a short journey, where you will be all alone. Make the best out of it.

"Dilkashi unn me naa thi, dekhne valo ki nigahon me ishq tha"

("The person wasn't attractive but the eyes of the beholder were brimming with love.")

ΔΔΔ

Part 1

THE QUESTION MARK?

Walking down the uneven path, the cold breeze brushed my face. It was January 4th, the snowfall in Kashmir made the temperature drop down to 7 degree Celsius. I was taking my regular rounds in the park. The wind was cold, I was shivering but the lump in my throat made me feel warm somewhere. I have lost the positivity. Disappointments cut deep. They make you bleed invisible blood. After all this time it wasn't 'Always', it was Him and Her.

Him – The unknown giving me the butterflies

&

Her – The one who told me to be firm and question everything.

I'll let you have the glimpses of my passing life. It had two main ingredients -Him & Her – Boiled to the core, with a pinch of salt and other spices.

Garnished with words and phrases.

Two months back, I was getting off the bus when our eyes met. He looked right in my eyes and said nothing. It was as if the months we had spent together were not important. It was as if nothing happened. He turned his back to me and entered the coffee shop. I followed him, when I pulled the glass door of the coffee house, I saw blood on my hands. I was taken aback. I didn't have the courage to go inside. I decided to have tea instead of my regular cup of coffee and went to a roadside tea stall. Unlike the clean and warm atmosphere of the coffee house, the roadside was noisy with the honking of vehicles, the smog was settling in, people were chattering loudly. The streetlights were getting illuminated. While sipping the tea, I felt my soul was resonating with all the noise and confusion. My daily encounters with him had left me ineffectual in my work life. Today felt a little different, I was much calmer than the rest of my days. I was thinking about my mother who had single-handedly managed the entire household and here I was struggling with myself. He was back again. My heart beats increased when I saw him with her, hand in hand lost in each other's eyes. I controlled my urge not to scream. They looked like they were so much in love. The woman's hair was curled down till her shoulders. She was wearing a mauve colored Velvet overcoat and black boots. The man had short hair and I could see his patchy beard. I

● ● ●

gasped for air. He was still running in my veins. Someone shoved against me and I fell down. Unknowingly, I had ventured into the Kids playing Arena. The Kids were rushing around me. I looked up, a little kid who had crashed into me turned around and said 'sorry' and ran away. A lady walked up to me and helped me get up on my feet again. She asked me if I was okay? Was I okay? I stared at the lady blankly not knowing what to say or do. I just nodded my head. The word 'sorry' tightened my gut. I could feel bile rising from my stomach. Did I bruise myself badly or were these memories hurting again? I was sorry and he was sorry. We both were sorry, but about what. Were we apologizing for our feelings or misunderstandings? I looked at the place where I saw them but the couple in front of me just disappeared like they got drifted away by mist. Yes, it was magical. It has to be magical or else it will be ordinary. Just like breathing and not living.

Struck by a plethora of darkness and wailing. My nights quaking with shivers and cold sweat down my nape. It's scary.

I stumble across your memories every hour, thinking if I would even ever see you again.

The pain I am growing through, Will it break my heart after 10 years?

I moved aside and sat on the bench thinking about the couple. The affection that I had just witnessed was something I had briefly experienced. Just like a flower pressed against the sheets of an old novel, the faint fragrant smell rose up to my nostrils and that's when I realized it had started drizzling.

The hopes, dream, and expectations shattering away with the large droplets of cold water on the ground. Some things are meant to fall, just like I was meant to fall for you.

It was all rainbows and unicorns. He was my happy place. After being desperate for love I saw that it is right in front of you, you just have to look carefully. More importantly, you need to identify the right one.

Love should be unconditional, apart from this everything should be conditional like respect and trust. Love for seeking the truth, and coming down to the truth what is it? Who knows?

We know the answer deep down within us; however, we always choose what is convenient for us.

Exploiting human strengths. Given the option, I would have traded all my tomorrows for your today.

My heart froze in winter
My love bloomed in spring
The monsoon nurtured my faith
And
In Autumn I fell for you...!

Brumal – The weather was now brumal-

Cuddle Weather. The cold never bothered me anyway. His presence was my mink blanket.

I couldn't stop you from walking away from me. I could only stretch my efforts so far like a rubber band before it came back and smacked me in the face. Getting hurt was my choice, better than breaking our bond. Was it my choice or you left me with no other option?

We take drastic measures for the things we care about.

Sitting here on the bench I know how many times your heart must be beating per minute right now.

Do I even know you now or did I ever know you?

My mind is overflowing with questions. We grow up thinking we will find answers. In our quest to seek answers, we end up having even more questions than before. Will this cycle ever stop?

I am fed up with the increase in question marks, filling me with anxiety and curiosity, maybe I was meant for something bigger. Oh, this uncertainty, this helplessness is seeping into my heart. The chaos in mind is screaming at me to silence it. Quite ironical you see.

One answer: I am waiting for the closure. Closure from people and things alike.

● ● ●

"*Hum unn ke alfazon mein ishq dhoondhte reh gaye, Aur who humari nigahon se mohabbat kar baithe*"

("*I tried searching for love in his words, little did I know that he had already fallen in love with my eyes.*")

ΔΔΔ

Part 2

THE DESCRIPTION.

I keep running away from the familiarity and end up looking at a mirror. The familiarity is hard to name. I see my reflection, the wavy hair which is always properly conditioned to make it smooth and voluminous. As I stare down at my hair, I can feel his long fingers playing with them. I can see him towering over me and gently whispering 'you are so beautiful. You are my lucky charm'. I give him a coy smile and hold his firm hands. I ask him, let's go out for dinner tonight? He hesitates a little but doesn't reply. He pulls me towards him by grabbing my waist. He gently caresses my face and I can feel his warm breath. My heart has started pounding loudly. I am sure he is able to hear my heartbeat. He touches his lips with mine and kisses me deeply. It feels like time has stopped and we are in some parallel Universe. It is only him and me. He sucks me deeper inside him. I can feel his hand under my t-shirt, reaching to unhook my bra. Bang!

Bang! I am woken up from my fantasy by someone banging the door. I look around myself, it is dark. He is nowhere to be seen. I fasten my footsteps as the banging increases. I opened the door and see a delivery man. My head throbbing in pain. I could feel my feet against the cold floor. It was raining heavily outside. His tall brooding body and everything else was there in my head that I could make out even in the darkness. His cuts and curves and his skin. I still wonder what he is… Is he a wizard or just a human who knows how to leave an impact on my mind? His deep voice taking my name still echoes in the house. The food that I had ordered was here. I had dozed off forgetting everything. Someone told me once that falling asleep would release the tension from your mind. I tell you clearly, it only releases tension when you are physically tired and not fatigued. I take my order and turn on the lights. I open the packets, luckily for me the food is still warm and edible. Any guesses what I ordered? yes, it's his favorite – Schezwan Pan-fried noodles. I pick up my fork to eat it and then slowly I see these noodles turn into worms and mud. I am unable to even take one bite. I walk down to the tap and drink the cold water. After splashing my face with water, I come back to my bed and close my eyes to sleep. The darkness in the room seems friendly to me. The environment is comforting.

This was different, the first time I saw him, I was the one gazing at him. He appeared like a night sky, full of stars, eyes symbolizing the charcoals, the fire blazing inside, neatly hidden under his calm composure.

He looked so calm and composed but his eyes were distant. His body was there but not his mind. You can easily capture the body but you cannot chain the soul.

Little did I know; he would burn me to ashes and chain my soul.

It started as a meeting of two strangers, I was immensely attracted to him. I looked down and cross-checked the message- the name, the place, and the table number. Something didn't feel right here. I approached the table. I saw the file with the word confidential written on it. Yes, this was indeed the guy for today. His eyes met mine and I felt a shiver down my spine. I told him my name and he smiled. Mind you all, the devil can appear innocent and charming and very attractive.

One meeting led to another and then to another. We kept meeting each other frequently, earlier for work-related purposes and then just to take our minds off from work-related stuff.

I loved him even though when it was quite clear we weren't supposed to be together. My Teacher told me to make mistakes and here I was making the biggest mistake of my life and didn't realize that it was a mistake until it was quite late. Apart from this, Mother told me many things like being courageous enough to show kindness to hatred, stand up for truth and be gentle with others. Fate introduced us for another purpose. I wish I could delete meeting you. Life isn't simple that way but is death comparatively simpler or easier?

It's difficult for me to walk away from my feelings. I used to think my mind is only a stubborn one but I realized my heart is stubborn too. A mere sight of you made my heart jump with joy. I meandered to a different fantasy world in my head.

Meeting you wasn't destiny since I have never believed in having one. Somebody who could strike you to your destiny, that's what I believed. I didn't know how to initiate a conversation with him, I completely forgot where I was. Drifting apart was destiny. It was cruel or maybe just confusing.

"Unki toh aadat thi, muskuraakar nazar faer lene ki... Chand lamha nigahen mila kar dil chura lene ki."

("It was customary of him/her to smile and quickly look away, few moments of our visual communication were enough for me to lose my heart away.")

I approached him and his eyes shot up and

looked at me questioningly. I pulled a chair and sat opposite to him. I wanted to hear his voice to make sure he was real. Little did I know his charming smile had cruelty hidden. His eyes which were quite deep like it had poison in them and oh! How desperate I was to have it all.

My love for you is like blood, it wants to beautify your soul's every fissure and crevices by covering it. You became my habit. One of the essentials needed for my survival.

Listing down the groceries of the week, I think about you. You neither wanted to be in my life nor I intended to stay. There were times I just stared at you and smiled; I want you to know that in those moments I was appreciating everything about you.

There are times when we need to talk or I have to say so much yet the words never come out, that time my pen bleeds on paper. There are times when we have to understand, yet we don't always know how. At our lowest times, during our toughest moments, things seem complicated and confusing. Leaving us to wonder, what the other is thinking or feeling. Often, we let pride get in the way and we lose the power and sense to communicate. I believe in us and all that we share. We have to open up and learn to give equally. I wish I could scream that I love you with all my heart.

"Crimson Red was my shade
Colored lips- his favorite
Peach pink on his collar pierced my heart apart."

It all started with a stained shirt, something which provided me with enough evidence to have doubts on you. The time stopped for me and my head started spinning. My world seemed to collapse in front of my eyes. It wasn't just a peach pink color; it was the beginning of turning my palette of colors into the shades of blacks and whites.

Colors – A tricky, subjective way to define our emotions.

If I could have been anything, I would have become the brightest color in the coloring box, instead, I chose him to decide the color of my cheeks, the color of my mind. The only thing that was mine was the crimson shade which I always wore on my lips, which was the reason his eyes first noticed me in a restaurant.

As the time elapsed the shade faded to become pink and then to peach-pink. What difference does the color make other than symbolizing my phases with you?

The loving phase - Crimson Red
The distance phase – Pink
The blow-up phase - Peach Pink

Somewhere among these colors, the mauve got lost. The deep rich mauve could be found nowhere except in my memories.

"The world was always colorful, it's that touch of kindness and magnanimity required to reflect the colors to the surface" – Kanika Verma

ΔΔΔ

Part 3

Mauve

A Poem.

We were a poem. An Allegory
Flowing in an anchored zone.
In the sunshine, our laughter echoed
Rhyming each other in every stanza
Never had I seen such artwork before.
We cannot have a rainbow, without the rain
We had our summer and had our frost
Now it's time to move away from this clock
Discovering a new measure will take us to our
new stop.
Met by fate, drifted by feat.
Learned to be strong and to be weak
All I essence is
An emblem of affinity can be clearly seen.

Mauve didn't convert itself into any brighter color instead it turned to darker shades for comfort.

Looking outside the window, the raindrops were tapping on the glass. We could hear the honks of the traffic and the clouds growling above. The rain felt sweet, refreshing, and nostalgic. I wanted to open the window and let the cool air enter our room. I looked at him, he was working on his laptop barely looking at me. I longed to be wrapped around in his loving arms. The distance cropped up; we tend to ignore the red flags. My career had hit rock bottom, I was not getting any assignments or now I think I didn't want to take. I was waiting for him to pop the question so that I could completely devote myself to him. Hope.

It can be a dangerous thing.
Love v/s Money.
They asked me: How close are you two?

I looked at them and smiled: Just look at him, he keeps me hidden in his wallet rather than in his heart. The bittersweet truth of relationships.

The Balance sheet.

Yes, He was working on his balance sheet.

His pen swiftly doing the complex calculations. The same fingers used to gently trace my skin, now trace someone else's body. He chose someone else, even though I gave him my everything. He had every piece of me and it hurts me every day.

His eyes glued on the screen
My eyes glistening with tears.

It is rare to find someone who never hurts you, we have to go for the one who is worth the pain.

The lack of judgement in us is the reason why we fall down in the ditch. Oh, this mistake was so grave that I didn't fall down, *I was buried.*

For him, I fought against the odds, went against my rules and struggled with my complexities.

If there were problems, we could have solved them. But you, my love, were a tragedy. Can anything go worse than this? Yes. I never got any closure. He was my longest project. Never had I imagined to stumble upon someone who could bring my life to an existential crisis.

Time passes but the memories are deep-rooted within. Even if you want, you can't totally erase it from your conscience.

In a different city, among different people, I am smiling and then his name pops up and the memories flood in.

How I was so naive,
so impressionable,
so vulnerable
at his mercy.

I pick up a book and start living the life of the characters. In the book, I travel every day from Ashbury to London, getting involved in disappearance and murder mystery. In between, I keep checking my cell phone expecting any message from him. Somewhere, I have this apprehension of never seeing any text from him.

"I am looking out of the window again, but I can feel his eyes on me and I have the oddest urge to turn towards him, to smell the smoke on his clothes and his breath. I like the smell of cigarette smoke. Tom smoked when we first met. It's erotic to me, that smell; it reminds me of being happy." – the lines took me back to him.

I was trying to break free from his memories. I sip the hot water from my cup and instantly the warmth of the water reminds me of his lips, soft and tender. I can smell his smoked breath. I can taste his mouth on me. I can feel his arms wrapped around me and him whispering "sweetheart" gently in my ear. That was erotic to me, that smell; the lines reminded me of being happy.

The novel opened my wounds. The night didn't do anything to make it better. If I had little more courage or strength within me, I would have chosen to turn this into something fruitful but alas, what did I do, I gave up on myself and there I lost the game.

You will go to any lengths to protect the ones you deeply love and care about and most of the time that person is someone else, not yourself. You end up saving them at the cost of destroying yourself.

Here I bleed again on paper.

I opened my heart in front of him.
Set my demons free.

And fell hard with no one to catch me. So, I crashed on the floor breaking the tiles of expectations.

Lying there…
Expressionless…
Emotionless.

The blisters on my hands for holding on too long.

Feeling the coldness of the broken tiles.
I believe, I bore what I never deserved.

Who can judge? Who can answer? Or with whom I can talk about.

That I killed
I killed the hope.
I killed our Child.
Numb.

The choices we make in life mold us into a particular person. They shape our future and challenge our insecurities.

ΔΔΔ

Part 4

The uncertainties engulfed me,
I feel like Alice tumbling down the Rabbit hole.

The pain can be exhilarating too. When you unshielded your trueness and bared yourself naked and people walk over you. You get stupefied by their ignorance of you. The art and beauty they had just witnessed are too much for their shaky hands.

Sometimes your own choices kill you rather than the circumstances.

I am sitting at a bus stop, waiting for love. I am looking down at the ground with my arms crossed and hearing the noise of ongoing traffic. I find that everything around me is moving, the world around me is constantly changing. Everyone is either coming or going somewhere. No one intends on staying. Here I am, having content in my eyes and calmness in my poise for the first-time notice that I am breathing. I count my breaths in a minute. My breaths were more than his heart beats per minute. I realized I had so much life and love in me which I was oblivious to all this time.

After all, we are made with the same ember as stars.

I was holding on with my hands when all I had to do was let 'him' go.

Just like an exciting movie, our lives have fun, struggle, depression, failure, a pinch of success, love, heartbreak, friendship, envy, comradeship, and we are the ones directing it. My part is to ensure it has a happy ending.

I had to accept that he was gone…

Somewhat the reason behind his disappearance was me.

What did he do to me?

Well, in short, he did not hug me when I was feeling low. He didn't feed chicken soup to me when I was sick. He didn't care that I waited for him late nights. He didn't notice me sobbing while sitting right in front of me during dinner.

He did one thing!

He made me feel miserable, and who gave that power to him, yes you are correct- I myself gave that power.

I can feel the eyes of strangers staring and passing remarks. They look at my high heels and mauve coat.

As I entered the office everyone gaped at me in astonishment. I walked confidently to my desk and settled down for the day's work.

• • •

My hair was no longer tied up in a bun,
the flowing hair had a tale to tell.

The bright lipstick was gushingly unapologetic about its bright cherry color. Yes, I changed the color- from Crimson to Cherry. This was a new me. Someone who was broken up in pieces and got built up again. Something had to change and yes it was the color. The sun was up and I was pure again.

I have my presentation at noon. My colleague comes to me and smiles and says 'Prepared for the big day. I smile and say 'yes'. The answer was 'yes', not just for office presentation but for the new me.

The stars failed to align on the astrological charts for a reason, they were pointing me towards the direction of making my own new sky.

We must unlearn the old and routine if we want to experience something new. At times, I end up questioning myself, how can something which is meant to nurture ends up destroying you. Being in love is good, but being blind can be dangerous if you are not looking, you'll get hit by the car. There is so much more to a book than the page you are stuck on. It is just a matter of perception one has towards life. It's not possible to be positive all the time but at least we can try.

Things turn around when you least expect them to. The entire Universe is constantly rhyming and in that our life is churning at its own pace. We try to channelize and understand it but we forget one simple thing, we cannot alter nature, even if we did, we are the ones who have to bear the consequences of it.

It's true that I had a life before all this and a sudden encounter with the events didn't alter the life which was flowing. It only affected the way I reacted to them. I let it out and then I am able to breathe the fresh air again. The dark lonely nights ended. There was a smile on my face – the warrior smile. It wasn't a physical fight that was fought, it had a lot to do about the emotional and mental phase that I was going about. It is all about turning the mundane things into something worthy. Worthy of your time and attention. Destiny plays its part and it will always be there but one thing I realized was- it has a lot more to do about how I react to it, the actions which I take.

If you are able to get up in the morning on time, that is an achievement for you. Others may think you are just enjoying or taking a break. It will suck you deeper into it. You got up in the morning when you felt like you don't know what to do with your day, where you want to go, what you want to achieve. That's a pretty good and brave step. No one will tell you this apart from you yourself or your therapist. It is only you who give power to the situations to take over you rather than you taking them over.

When we are in high spirits we tend to take decisions and stubborn people like us believe in it, even though it is just a figment of our imagination.

The presentation was a success. I wanted to treat myself with Caramel Frappuccino. I signaled my department-in-charge and went on a 20-min break. As I walked out of the building, the cool winter air caresses my face. I cross the road and I am welcomed by the aroma of the coffee beans. I close my eyes and feel at peace.

The Morning Coffee

Stirred ambition/like lava in me.
Like the world was waiting for me.
The morning sun reminding me
 To rise again.
To shine again.
And burn again.
I am ready to take my flight.
Absconding from the lies.
Escaping the shadows of echoes and
becoming a voice again.

We keep losing someone but the worst loss is when we lose ourselves to the circumstances. We all make mistakes, killing a child for the sake of gaining attention.

Some things are invisible, you can only see them with your eyes closed.

I sit with my coffee, looking out of the window. The world is busy as it has always been. It doesn't miss if few of the humans who were common in that area aren't seen. The world churns in chaos and activity in the hope of something exciting and new the day has to offer it. I see a park full of people, little kids are swinging and are on slides. Older folk is taking evening strolls at their own pace. The birds are returning back to their homes in flocks and a young couple is sitting under a tree and watching the sunset. Life seems to be full of joy, peace, and tranquility and somewhere in a corner, the death is lurching. Picking the person, it will devour next. As I was carried away in thoughts, I notice a movement around me - A girl wearing a black sweatshirt comes and sits across my table. I look at her and I say "you are late." She offers to buy me another cup to which I reply "Let's paint our souls with color tonight. Deeper, darker and sweeter." she gives a playful wink. The deal is sealed but fate is not.

I slide a couple of sheets across the table for her to sign. I look into her eyes and ask if she is sure about this.

I have learned this thing - Be so convincing that they believe that storms are there to wash you clean.

• • •

She doesn't respond, making me anxious, I quietly sip my coffee and watch her read the lines. She picks up the pen on the table and signs it.

Like this, I get another approval.

Have you ever heard anyone say that the job of being a contract murderer is easy?

Yes, that's correct, I was trained to murder making it look like accidents. It all started with a childhood game where I along with other kids was forced to do things that were unethical perhaps illegal. Initially, we played it for money, it was a disappearing act. In the hustle and bustle of the city, nobody notices the missing bodies. The beauty of this was we never saw anyone known who got disappeared. We were smiling and giggling kids running here and there.

ΔΔΔ

Part 5

Earlier we did it for sweets later we did it for money.

I was rescued or should I say I found my escape. I always found peace in reading and writing. We were enrolled in schools so that it looks like the people who were taking care of us could provide justification for the acts. I rarely made friends because children were moved away from one home to another. We were a few selected children who were trained to become this.

My Mother

She was this frail lady with a streak of silver hair.
She is never aged in front of our eyes.
Her laugh would brighten the room.
Her eyes would sparkle and bravery would reflect.
The surreal relation that I had in the darkness.
The one who protected me from the master/ teacher.

*The one who always said - Masters will come and
go
but life is the biggest teacher if not the greatest.
She asked me to respect my teacher.
I Didn't know she wanted me to run away far
from here.
Naively I followed the instructions of my human
master.
Unaware that the world is cruel, manipulative
and sadist.
O mother, o my sweet mother
I Wish I could make you proud one last time.*

We were told we were special and have a goal
to fulfill in life- to serve the benefit of the
community. Mother was different, she was there
to protect us. She was scared of the master but
still, she didn't run away. We think that fighting,
objecting and protesting is brave, but being brave
is to endure whatever life throws at you and you
accept it with a smiling face. Every night I would
listen to the sobbing voice coming from her room,
We were not allowed to get up from our beds even
if we heard screams or cries. The next morning, I
would see her greeting us smilingly as we spoke
our morning prayers before breakfast. I asked her
about the cries but she never disclosed the reason
behind it.

We could always feel the master's eyes on us.
He somehow knew every little thing we used to
do. Discipline and obedience were the most

important thing for him. He had no room under his shelter for those with the rebel in their eyes.

Somewhere in a corner, the mother was watering a plant so that it could grow stronger and greener than the rest of the others. She always came to me in the evening and used to say '*Bachha*, don't forget to write today.' I felt it weird and strange but at the end of the day I always felt if I don't write, I am missing something major in life and my day is incomplete without it.

The first time I entered the computer room, I was nervous. I was told it will be a fun activity. We were asked to remove our shoes and sandals. There was a Man with big spectacles and mustache standing beside the Master. His shirt was crumpled and his feet were smiling. There were devices in front of us which I later learned were called computers. We were five children. He looked at us and ask us to tell him our favorite words. When my turn came, I nervously replied 'Chai' (tea). Then he made all of us recite all the alphabets and started quickly scribbling down a few notes. The session was never-ending, I was hungry. Finally, in the evening we were let out of the room. I wondered why we were not allowed to do anything with those machines. As I came outside, I saw mother talking to another worker on a compound like the harvesting has started, the kids are being trained to do what they shouldn't be involved in. Mother saw me and gave me a cold stare. Instead of being hustled in kids' dormitories, we were moved to another building. There we were kept in one room. For dinner, we were brought to the kitchen. The carpet was rolled out and we were asked to finish our food quickly.

When it was time for bed, I realized, I had forgotten my writing notebook and pencil. I looked out of the window; the view was peaceful.

The crescent moon was shining brightly,
The stars scattered across the sky.
The entire world gazed at it in awe.
The perfect image cast upon the waters below,
The rippling of the waves deciding the perfect filter.
The moon smiled while clicking her own picture every night.
Teaching us to fall in love with her every night.

I got drifted away from mothers in the coming days. The man who was training us to write and operate computers was the only one with whom we were engaging in conversations. The cooks and the workers barely spoke to us.

One day the man did not come and were told to join the kids in the other area. When we reached there, many new faces looked at us.

I went to the mother smilingly and she greeted me back and started filling me with the news of the compound. She asked me to meet her later in the evening under the mango tree, before going back.

The mother looked weak; the grey hair strands were clearly visible. I was already sitting under the tree, I had befriended loneliness. She came to me and asked if I was feeling okay. She said I brought you a gift and handed me my notebook and pencil.

She looked at me and told me that I should find an escape from this web.

The bell rang. It was my time to say goodbye to her.

I had forgotten how much I missed her soothing voice. I used to think that I will become like her when I grew up. Looking after the kids who the world had long forgotten. The world was getting smaller and was choking us all in the empty space.

One thing was familiar even though it went through phases and changed its shape every night:

Moon.
Darling,
Dark night,
Glistening sky...
I look up not to see any star,
but my moon illuminating the night sky.

The count of children in the compound was less than what was before. It grew smaller in the coming days. More Children were enrolled in the typing. We became fast friends, the privilege we didn't have in the compound. We had to maintain silence and discipline. Boys and girls were kept separately which later became evident why.

Our proper schooling started; we were taught various subjects. I thoroughly enjoyed the wonders of science, the puzzle of the number, long ballads in literature.

One day we were told to pack our belongings early in the morning and were asked to stand in a line.

I saw Mother after months. I saw a sadness in her eyes. She was giving all of us packed food and water bottle. It was clear they were taking us away. When my turn came, I wanted to sit with her and talk to her about things for hours. She was in no mood to talk, nor were the surroundings.

While handing the stuff to me she said:

"Run somewhere far from here, do not trust anyone, trust yourself- Fight and Survive."

On the bus, I kept on thinking about her. She asked me to do things which she wasn't able to do.

Some things are in plain sight but we entangle it into complexity rather than understanding its simplicity. We often discover it late in life. Your search for answers, the meaning of life, love, courage, and motivation.

The trick is simple - to keep eyes open and observe your environment – happiness and suffering alike.

Know more about the world today than you knew yesterday!

He and Mother used different words but meant the same thing - 'Spark up your soul and fly high as long as you are alive.'

The nights were filled with violence and screaming. When people were in the safety of homes, the massacre, the cold that nibbled our skin and soul alike made us cruel with our intentions.

I never thought that I could run away from all this. Few tried, never saw them again. I wondered where had the rest of the people vanished.

The mother had asked me to run away when I had the chance, one mistake and it was over for me. Snap and gone!

Everything you want is on the other side of the Fear or it is the end.

After deboarding the bus, we were hustled into hostels. We were put into separate rooms and allotted different colleges. It was a new world. Each of us was given a person to whom we had to report at the end of the day. We were asked to spy on people. He was my assignment that went horribly wrong.

He was called 'Subject' and the task was to isolate and overpower him. Someone wanted him dead.

All the time Mother was warning me about this day. A day would come when I will not have a choice.

Monsters are real and they look like people, just like you and me.

I close my eyes again and lie down quietly in my coffin. I lied down in the graveyard with Mother's grave in another corner of the same cemetery. His dead body was burnt to ashes. I never knew I was destined to become fatal for him. I longed to be burnt in the fire which burnt him rather I was the one who ignited the fire.

Yes, I was dead but the nightmares lived and they lived forever.

Sunrise.

Many people want to talk about it but very few get up that early to feel the mesmerizing light and warmth of it to sink in their bones.

ΔΔΔ

Epilogue

You must be wondering this book talks about the past, we are what our circumstances made us and the choices we made to deal with the situation at that time.

The reason is we look into the past to fetch the answers for the present and future. Scientifically, historically we try to find the causes, effects, and reasons. Mostly we find all these answers within our past. How we have been made, the way we think, our little habits define us and make us what we are today. We fail to recognize it. It was my attempt to make this fiction a metaphor of our reality that surrounds and grips us. Much of the events that take place in our lives are consequences of our decisions and thoughts that we put in; one thing leads to the other. Selfishness can be positive or negative. The tendency of being too selfish creates negative energy around us. The book starts with the gloominess, sadness but the energy can be transformed into something positive, the day you have truly said ENOUGH to all the negative energy around you.

Ashwani Kujur

Be the warrior! Treat every other day as another day to be alive before you get buried deep in mud.

ΔΔΔ

Acknowledgement

I could not possibly have completed this book without the help of many people in my lives. The people I treasure the most in the world- My family (Maa & Papa) and friends.

I used to write short poems or quotes or *shaayari* since school time, it never occurred to me that I can write a book, but these individuals encouraged me. Thank you for believing in me when I was doubtful. Thank you to my college sisters who are far and busy hustling but are just one phone call away. Not naming anyone here but I would like to thank each of them for all the support they have given me. Writing a book is harder than I thought, on this note, I would like to thank Raunak Agarwal – without him I would have never finalized or gone through all the hassles to produce this piece.

ΔΔΔ

About the Author

Graduated and somehow survived commerce, Ashwani Kujur has more curls in her hair than in her thinking. Born in Jharkhand but brought up in Delhi, she drinks, chews, snorts, and operates on caffeine - the aroma which she considers a must to silence her thoughts. She also claims to be lethargically motivated, drawn like a moth to a flame to anything that physically or mentally exhausts her.

Eternally stuck between thriving to exercise and her cravings for French fries and Ice cream, you can get in touch with her below:

1. Instagram – ashwanikujur

2. Facebook – ashwini.kujur

3. Snapchat – Ash10i

You can also email her for any questions: ashwanikujur10@gmail.com

ΔΔΔ